Go to Sleep, Little Groundhog

Claude Clément
Adapted by Patricia Jensen
Illustrations by Catherine Nouvelle

Reader's Digest Young Families, Inc.

As the first snowfall arrived in the mountains, the animals prepared for the long winter ahead. Families snuggled together in burrows and caves and started getting ready to sleep. Everyone except one groundhog family, that is. They were busy looking for their littlest groundhog.

The little groundhog was still outside
because she wanted to play a while longer.
She romped up the hill with her friend the goat.
"My little groundhog," her mother called.
"Please come into the burrow right away!
It's time to go to sleep."

"Oh, Mama!" the little groundhog begged.
"Just a few more minutes! After I play a bit,
I'm sure I'll feel like going to sleep."

"Five more minutes," said her mother.
"Then it's bedtime."

So off the little groundhog went.

Five minutes passed, but the little groundhog still showed no signs of getting tired.

Her weary mother asked the ermine for advice.

"I know just the thing to help your little groundhog go to sleep," he said confidently.

Just then, the little groundhog bounced in, full of energy.

"Come, little groundhog, wrap your tail around yourself like this," said the ermine. "Why, I'm getting sleepy already," he yawned.

"My tail isn't long enough to wrap around myself," the puzzled little groundhog said.

The ermine sighed. "I hadn't thought of that. Wait here. I'll be back in a minute with someone who can help you."

The ermine dashed out of the burrow into the snow to find his friend the lizard. Meanwhile, the little groundhog huddled in the burrow, wide awake.

"The little groundhog can't fall asleep? I'll show her exactly what to do," said the lizard after hearing the ermine's story. "It's easy and it works every time."

And with that, the lizard and the ermine scurried off to the groundhogs' burrow.

The little groundhog greeted the lizard happily. "Are you here to play with me?" she asked.

"Oh, no," said the lizard. "We've got work to do. Now, falling asleep must be taken very seriously. Just lie completely still—don't move a muscle!"

The little groundhog tried to stay still, but it was just too hard. "Lizard," she whispered. "How long before I fall asleep?"

But the lizard didn't answer. He was too busy snoring.

Just then a rabbit hopped in. "Hello, little groundhog," he said. "I heard you're having trouble falling asleep. The trick is to count twitches."

"Twitches?" asked the little groundhog. "Like twitching my nose?"

"Exactly!" said the rabbit. So together they twitched noses, counting every twitch. But before they even got to ten, the rabbit was sound asleep.

The little groundhog's parents closed their weary eyes to think. "What shall we do?" her father asked her mother. "We simply must get some rest."

Before her mother could answer, there was a knock at the entrance to the burrow. There, shivering in the cold, stood a tiny cricket.

"I'm sorry to bother you," the cricket began. "Do you have a warm spot for me inside your burrow? In exchange for your kindness, I will be happy to play some songs for you."

The groundhog family quickly welcomed the poor cricket into their snug burrow. Once he warmed up, he began to rub his wings together to play a lively tune.

In a flash, the lizard and the rabbit woke up. Soon everyone in the burrow was dancing and singing merrily.

Everyone but the little groundhog, that is.
She was curled up in the corner, fast asleep!

The cricket continued chirping as the guests danced their way out of the burrow and back to their homes. Then the groundhog family quietly snuggled around the little groundhog and happily closed their eyes for their long winter nap.

"Good night, little groundhog," the cricket chirped softly.

During the summer, groundhogs like to eat grass and roots. They eat so much that they are able to survive the long winter without having to search for food.

In winter, groundhogs snuggle in their burrows to sleep until the following spring.

Groundhogs' burrows are underground tunnels with many entrances and little rooms. Before leaving the burrow, a groundhog will poke his head up to make sure there is no danger outside.